LIVE AND LET GROW

PENNY REID

WWW.PENNYREID.NINJA/NEWSLETTER/

COPYRIGHT

PART ONE

ALICE

"I'm doing it!"

"Alice—"

"No." I jabbed a solitary finger in the air. "No, Jackie. You listen to me. Do you hear that?"

"Hear what?"

"The determination in my voice? The lack of doubt? That's the sound of willpower. I'm doing it this time. I'm in it to win it."

"Oh, Alice." Even through the phone I could detect the sympathy, the worry, the compassion, and perhaps just a wee bit of exasperation.

"Don't you 'Oh, Alice' me. Milo is coming home tomorrow, and I'm ready for him this time. I'm so ready. I wrote a letter." A letter which I'd already placed on his kitchen table along with a new houseplant—an anthurium, which had heart-shaped leaves. I'd wondered if the symbolism was a little too on the nose, but oh well. Too late now. He loved plants, and I loved him.

The day had come, and I was seizing it!

"A letter," my sister said, like leaving a handwritten love letter wasn't one of the most revolutionary things someone could do. I felt like a Bolshevik, a real radical, just . . . you know. Less murdery.

"Yes! A letter!" Spinning in a circle, I took one more look at Milo's apartment to ensure all was as it should be and then skipped to his bathroom.

When he left on his months-long work trips, I was his designated plant-watcher and mail picker-upper. I also ran his sinks and flushed his toilets because dry sewer pipes sometimes stank, and prolonged stagnant water is never a good thing.

Sometimes I'd hang out in the apartment on my own, reading books or working. I loved his apartment. It felt like being with Milo but without constantly having to fight the eruption of butterflies every time our eyes met or we touched. Or he laughed. Or smiled. Or spoke. *Or breathed.*

Point was, I felt close to him here, even when he was gone. Large photographic art prints hung on the walls, remote and beautiful places he'd visited and told me about upon his return. His décor, the colors, were all cool and relaxing—sand, pebble gray, stone blue—and no matter how long he'd been gone, the bathroom always smelled faintly of his aftershave.

"So, you're leaving a letter, exactly like the last time," came my sister's flat voice. She paired it with a sigh.

"No." I ceased sniffing the bathroom and flipped off the light. "This is completely different. Like I said, this letter is *handwritten*. I can't hack into his email server and delete it from his inbox this time, or hack into his Facebook account and remove it from his personal messages. Or hack into his Instagram, or his—"

"Yes. I know. I was present each time to watch over your shoulder because you wanted a witness to watch you *not* look at or read any of his other messages. What night should I keep free so I can watch you do it again."

It's true. My sister had been in the room with me each of the other eleven times. She'd watched me get in, delete my message, and get out. And yes, I realize hacking into anyone's personal accounts is an extreme violation of privacy, which is why I'd told Milo about each of the hackings.

I'd say, "Milo, I hacked into your Instagram account last night and deleted a message I sent you. Jackie was there to ensure I didn't look at anything else."

And he'd say, "Okay," and shrug those broad shoulders, a quizzical-looking smile on his handsome lips, his green, sparkly eyes unconcerned because he trusted me. Then he would offer me wine, which I always turned down. When we spent time together, he was always drinking wine and I was always turning it down, but he continued to offer.

It's not that I didn't like wine. I did. A lot. I drank it when we went out with other people, when it was more than just the two of us. I just didn't want to drink wine in Milo's apartment when it was just me and him. Sober, I was honest, but not too honest. Like how some people show their ID when buying alcohol even though the checkout person probably wasn't going to ask for it? That was me when I drank, but instead of an unsolicited ID, I handed over honesty.

I supposed, after fifteen years of friendship, Milo's trust was warranted. Also, he knew I was a weirdo. So . . .

"So, tonight? Tomorrow?" My sister no longer attempted to conceal her exasperation. "When should I be available for your inevitable panic attack?"

"You're not listening, Jackie. I can't hack a piece of paper." Picking up my coat from the couch where I'd draped it, I balanced my cell against my shoulder and shoved my arms through the sleeves.

"Okay, paper. Wow. But what's going to keep you from ripping it up ten minutes before he arrives? You've had a key to his place forever."

"Ah-ha!" I pulled my key ring out of my coat pocket and, still balancing the phone between my shoulder and jaw after adjusting for my coat, I unclipped his key. "I've thought of everything. You see, after one has chickened out eleven times, outsmarting oneself is difficult, but not impossible."

"In English, please."

"I'm leaving the note *inside* his apartment."

She made a small sound of weariness. "You're talking in circles. I don't see how this makes a difference. You. Have. A. Key."

"But I'm slipping the key under his door so I can't sneak back inside and destroy the letter before he sees it." While I said the words, I walked out of Milo's apartment, shut the door, locked the dead bolt, and slipped the key under the door. *There. All done.* Man, that felt good.

"This time I'm serious. No backing out. No take-backsies. I might be a coward, but I am a persistent, determined coward."

"Okay. Okay. I see you've thought this out. But Alice . . ." I heard her shift in her seat or maybe stand. "You are my sister, and you know I love you."

"Yes. I know. I love you." Marching down the hall away from Milo's door, I stood tall and proud. This was it. *This is it! GAH!*

"And you know I think Milo is hot and charming and brilliant."

"You think he's hot?" I paused at the door leading to the stairwell. He lived on the third floor of a twenty-five-floor building. I always took the stairs.

"Sorry. Sometimes his hot professor vibe is all I see," my sister said. "He seems like a lovely, lovely person. But he's also hot."

I guess Milo was hot. Actually, no. He was definitely hot.

But on the list of reasons of why I loved Milo, his hotness was not even in the top ten. He was hilarious, often when I least expected it, stealthy, catching me off guard. He was smart—*so smart*—and loved to learn. He loved to share what he learned. I never grew tired of talking to him, and we always had too much to talk about; our evenings together often ran past midnight.

Also, he liked me for me. He seemed to sincerely enjoy my company and value my opinion. He asked me questions and always seemed interested in my responses, even when it took me a half hour to explain the context for my answer before I gave it.

And, yes, in eleventh place, he possessed an extremely pleasing exterior: jade green eyes with starbursts of gold, dark black lashes and dark brown curly hair on top of a face with sharp cheekbones and a square jaw. He'd rowed in college and kept up with it, even now owning an ergometer. He also climbed mountains and scaled the sides of cliffs whenever he traveled.

But it was his smile I loved the most out of all his physical attributes. There was just something about it; when he laughed with abandon, that made me feel like I was floating and my heart had wings. Oh, how I loved his smile.

"Okay, sure," I conceded. "I guess Milo is hot. So what?"

"Therein lies my main concern."

I frowned, trying to think through her words and discover the hidden meaning. My sisters—and other people—did this. Ultimately, speaking in code was why my ex-husband and I had divorced. But he wasn't the weird one, I was. *I* was the problem. I understood now that humans spoke in code, hoping I would pick up on some underlying message so they wouldn't have to say whatever it was out loud. It annoyed me to no end. *Why can't people just say what they mean?*

"Are you saying you think he's too hot for me?" I switched my phone from my right hand to my left.

"No. I think he's too hot for anyone. Hot guys like Dr. Milo Manganiello are genetically incapable of relationships."

"Genetically incapable?"

"Yes. It's a defect in their DNA."

"Ha ha." She had to be joking. I pushed open the stairwell door.

"Okay. Listen to me. Take Will, for instance."

"What does Will have to do with anything?" My fingers skimmed over the rail as I descended. My ex-husband and I got along fine whenever we crossed paths, which wasn't often. But it was unavoidable since we worked for the same university.

"Will is super hot, always has been. And why did you and he get a divorce? Because he couldn't stop having sex with—"

"So what?" I wanted to argue with Jackie, tell her that the real reason for our split was because Will spoke in code and I didn't. Communication had been our downfall. His infidelity was just the symptom.

"So I've dated hot guys before too. I just broke up with a hot guy. It's always the same, isn't it? And there are more red flags than just what Milo looks like. He's almost forty, and he's never been married."

My feet stalled on the first landing and I leaned my shoulder against the wall. "You're thirty-eight, and you've never been married."

"It's different for women and you know it. When was the last time he had a girlfriend?"

"A girlfriend?" My voice cracked. I noticed a chip of paint on the wall. I turned away from it.

"Doesn't he tell you about all his girlfriends?" she asked, even though she already knew the answer.

"He doesn't date, Jackie. But you know that already. And you know why. With all his traveling and work, it doesn't make sense."

"Yes. You're right. Milo dating doesn't make sense, especially when he has you there, watering his plants and waiting for him whenever he comes home." A growly edge entered her voice. "You don't think he's hooking up with people on these trips? Come on. Hot professor traveling the world? You are naïve, but you can't be *that* naïve."

A sick feeling settled in my stomach. "I guess I am that naïve," I admitted quietly, not needing to contemplate the level of my naïveté.

Not only was I naïve, I was a sucker, gullible in the extreme. I took things too literally; I knew this about myself. It was why—after so many painful experiences in my twenties—I avoided making new friends and remained suspicious and guarded with new people for years before trusting them. But after so many years of friendship, I didn't think I needed to be on guard with Milo.

In the past, even during my marriage to Will, when I'd check in and ask Milo if he was seeing anyone, he'd say, "You know I don't have time for relationships," and then he'd make a face.

But that wasn't really an answer, was it? *Maybe that was code for something else?* But no. Milo didn't use code with me. He was one of the few people I could count on to just say what he meant.

"All I'm saying is, think this through," she said. "You two are good friends. You know he doesn't date. And you're going to confess that you *love* him? Do you want to lose him as a friend?"

"Of course not." I rubbed my chest with my fingertips. The sick feeling had spread to my lungs. I swallowed around something rough and thick, crossing the arm not attached to the phone over my stomach. "Why didn't you say something before now? You know how I—you know how I've felt about him for years."

My sister must've been standing because I heard footsteps and then a click, like a door closed. "I didn't say anything at first—none of us did—because he was a good friend to you when you were going through your divorce."

I nodded, biting the inside of my lip. Milo and I had met in college. He'd been a physics grad student and I'd been a computer science undergrad. He'd needed a tutor for a programming class, and I was a volunteer with the comp sci department. Tutoring looked good on grad school applications, but I also volunteered because it was one of the only—and most effective—ways I'd been able to make friends in college.

Milo and I did become friends. *Good* friends. Will and I were engaged at the time, but Will went to school on the West Coast. Milo and I would go out for coffee, go out to dinner, be each other's friend-date to parties. He'd been at my wedding to Will and, ten years later, he'd taken me out to dinner the night my divorce had been finalized. I wanted to think, first and foremost, Milo Manganiello and I would *always* be friends.

"I was honestly really impressed with him after your divorce, keeping you company, helping you stay busy, going on that trip with you to Montreal. He was such a sweetheart."

Now I made a sound of distress, and my eyes lifted to the stairway door I'd just passed through, one landing up. "Then why are you saying he's a jerk now?"

"No. I didn't say hot guys are jerks, I'm telling you they're rarely, if ever, monogamous. And as long as they're upfront about it, then that's not jerky. But we're getting off topic. The reason I never said anything after the divorce is because you two were really good friends, and you needed a good friend. But then you started . . ."

"What?"

"You started having feelings for him, or saying you did, and I thought that was great. You needed to move past your ex. Will had been your high school boyfriend, your college boyfriend, and then your husband. You've never been with anyone but him. Showing interest in Milo was a good thing . . . two years ago."

"I was with Will for almost seventeen years. Two years doesn't seem like such a long time to me."

"Except you're thirty-six now, and you've only had *one* relationship. You've been stuck on this one guy for two years. Haven't you wasted enough of your life? Don't you want to get out there and start living?"

"That's why I wrote the letter on paper this time." I gestured wildly to nothing. "I'm trying to—I need to tell him how I feel."

"Why?"

"You know why."

"Because you're in love with him? Because you won't give anyone else a chance? Because your life—a life you fought hard for—is slipping away because you can't get over a guy who is never going to see you as anything but a really good friend?"

Ugh. Now my stomach hurt. "You don't know that."

"No, I don't. But I've been through heartbreak, more than once, and it sucks. *You've* been through an epic heartbreak too. Think of what happened with Will. If

I can protect you from that, from the destruction of another unrequited love with a hot guy, I will." She sighed, sounding tired. "So before you plant the letter and slip the key under his door, think about this. REALLY think about it. You two are best friends. Best friends for fifteen years."

"Yes. I know. And you know I love him."

"Yes. He also clearly loves you too. As. A. Friend."

"Or he just needs a little push?" I asked hopefully.

"Or he's an almost-forty, hot professor in his prime who travels all over the world and isn't ever going to be ready to settle down, even with you. And you're fucking amazing! It's not you. It's him."

"Jac—"

"Hasn't he told you over and over that he doesn't do relationships? Now you're going to ask him to try with you? No, girl. No. Don't you believe if Milo had feelings for you—any romantic feelings whatsoever—he would've brought them up by now?"

"Ugh, that's another good point." My stomach filled with dread. *Great. Now I have a doom stomachache.*

"And what about all the times he's tried to set you up with his friends since your divorce?"

I grimaced, the hand holding my stomach moving to my forehead. "He hasn't tried to set me up, he's—" I didn't know what to call it.

Milo had never suggested I date any of his friends. Not exactly. More like, he'd say, "Are you open to dating someone yet?" and I'd say, "I don't think so." And he'd say, "Promise me you'll let me know if you're ever interested, I'll set you up."

I would always feel a little squicky afterward, off-balance, confused. And sad. Really sad. I think Milo assumed I wasn't yet ready to get back out there after the divorce. Little did he know I'd never wanted to "get back out there" because I was head over heels for him.

My stomach twisted, and a rising something burned my esophagus. "I—I think I'm going to be sick."

"Don't do it."

"I'll try not to throw up, but Jackie—"

"Tear up the letter."

"I can't—"

"Go out with that PhD candidate from the literature department who keeps hinting about taking you to a concert. He might not be Will or Milo hot, but he has gorgeous eyes. What's his—"

"No. Jackie! I—I already shut the door!"

"Uh, what?"

"The door. I shut it. I shut the door." I didn't know what to do. Did I go back to his apartment and try to fish the key out from under the door?

"Well, open the door!"

"I can't. I left the key inside."

"Oh no."

"It's inside. And I'm outside!" I lifted my hand toward the landing above me. The distance between me and that letter might as well have been Mount Everest.

"What are you going to do?" The question was breathless.

"I'll—I'll ask the super to let me in." *Where is the super?* I'd met her once. She was nice. She had a cat, and it liked me.

"Alice."

My feet were already flying down the stairs. I was pretty sure she lived on the first floor. "I'm sure she'll—"

"Let you into one of her tenants' apartments? Sure."

"What else can I do?" I gripped the railing to keep from slipping as I took a stair too fast.

Jackie was silent for a long time. A long, long time.

So long I asked, "Jackie? Did you hang up?"

"I'm here."

"I can't hack into an apartment." I groaned.

"No. You can't."

"What can I do?"

"Pray."

PART TWO

MILO

I typically flew standby on international flights. If I was lucky—a phenomena closely correlated to the airline ticket agent's level of flirt-susceptibility—I'd be assigned an aisle or a window. If I was really lucky, I'd be given a spot next to an empty seat. Once every five trips or so, I'd be upgraded to first or business class. In these cases, I would also end up with the ticket agent's phone number. Always unsolicited, but a nice boost to the ego, nevertheless.

This time my ticket agent had been Tori from Bristol, or so her name tag informed me. She hadn't looked old enough to be a ticket agent, so I hadn't attempted to flirt with her.

Sandwiched between a husband and wife who weren't willing to compromise on giving up his aisle seat or her window—i.e., they'd booked travel with a seat between them—the pair seemed irritated that the spot had been given to me, a tall dude of unspecified origin in dirty traveling clothes. They'd both assumed I didn't speak English for the first hour of the trip. The woman thought I was Egyptian and the man contended that I was clearly Pakistani.

By hour two, tired of their debate, I announced with a smile, "Hi. I'm Milo, first-generation Italian American. My parents are from Italy, but I was born in Iowa. I teach physics at a university in New York. What's your name?"

Mercifully, after quick introductions, they were quiet, if not a little put out that I'd neglected to announce my ancestry while we were taxiing at Heathrow. The flight wasn't the worst I'd ever experienced, nor the best.

But it will all be worth it.

Thoughts of Alice, of seeing her after so many weeks away, kept me up on the plane instead of sleeping. She wouldn't come by tonight; she rarely did on my first day back, insisting I rest. But I could count on seeing her tomorrow, most likely in the morning for breakfast and coffee. Every once in a while, she'd wait until lunch, but I'd definitely see her for dinner at the very, very latest. She would want to give me a tour of the houseplants, tell me about their progress as though they were pets or employees instead of greenery.

I loved it, and I couldn't wait. She'd always end up laughing, enduring my teasing with a good-natured acceptance, and Alice's laugh was contagious. Then we'd make plans for the weekend and we'd settle into our normal rhythm: breakfast on campus every day, lunch when she had time, and dinner Thursday through Sunday.

Finally, the plane landed, and I immediately checked my phone, smiling when I spotted her text.

Alice: Did you land yet?

I quickly typed a response.

Milo: Just landed. Will I see you for breakfast tomorrow?

Alice: Hopefully before that.

My grin widened at her reply, hoping that meant she'd be coming over tonight after my nap. Before I could respond, I became aware that both the husband and wife on either side of me were reading over my shoulder.

"Wife?" the woman asked.

I forced a polite smile, a non-answer. People on planes were always trying to set me up with their sister or daughter or niece's roommate's yoga instructor. This was the excuse I used for keeping a picture of Alice as my lock screen and another of the two of us as my background. Turning my phone slightly, I showed Alice's picture to the woman.

"Oh, she's stunning." As we taxied to the gate, the woman patted my arm. "Is she a model? Actress?"

I wasn't surprised by her guesses. People always thought she was an actress when I showed them this picture. "No. Professor of computer science."

"Really?" She flinched back, clearly surprised. "How long have you two been together?"

"A long time." As far as I was concerned, we *had* been together a long time, just not in the way the woman meant.

"Any kids?"

I shook my head, turning the phone back to me, admiring the picture of Alice, the honest openness of her gaze, the symmetry of her gorgeous face, the curve of her slightly parted lips, the glow of her skin.

I swallowed the dizzy longing, turning the phone off and rubbing my eyes.

Alice didn't let me take photos of her often and typically made a silly face when I tried. The one on my lock screen was one of the very few I had where her eyes weren't crossed. This photo was my favorite.

I'd snapped the photo last summer. We'd just returned from the city pool and she'd taken a shower.

Her hair was down around her shoulders, almost dry, and her cheeks were still flushed, pink from the sun. She wore a white tank top and yoga pants and was making tea. Alice was always making tea, even when it was hot outside. I pretended to clean my camera as I watched her from the kitchen table.

Alice blew the steam off the surface of the teacup, her lips forming a plush little 'O' and my stomach tightened. I'd had trouble breathing. Automatically, I lifted the camera, waiting for the right moment, framing her. She took a sip, licked her lips, and lowered the cup. Her eyes lifted. She looked at me.

And I took my shot.

She immediately made a face and turned away. But it didn't matter, I had what I wanted.

Presently, the woman next to me clicked her tongue. "No children? You don't want to have children with her?"

"I would love to have children with her," I responded easily and laughed inwardly at myself. I had an easier time telling a strange woman on a plane how I felt than I did talking to my best friend. How's that for irony?

Now the lady tsked mournfully, giving me a once-over and frowning. "But she doesn't? Focused on her career?"

I glanced at the woman, finding her eyebrows raised expectantly, judgment written in her features.

She twirled a finger in the direction of my torso and face as she said, "You two would have beautiful children."

"Leave him alone, Poppy," the husband grumbled, leaning forward to talk over me. "And get your carry-on out. We have a connecting flight."

Thankfully, before she could make another comment, the captain came on with an announcement and then we were all standing, grabbing our carry-ons and departing the plane.

An hour later, I was stumbling into my building's elevator, not quite able to remember the ride home. *I should've slept on the plane.* I leaned my head against the side of the wall and sighed, waiting for the old pulley system to engage. Usually, I would take the stairs, but not with all the bags and the lack of sleep.

Finally reaching my floor, I kicked my duffel bag into the hallway. I wanted a shower and water and—

"Milo."

Startled, my head whipped up, and I had to blink several times before I could believe my eyes. "What—" I grinned automatically as I looked her up and down, heat warming and tightening my chest as I pushed the remainder of my bags off the elevator with my foot. "Alice. What are you doing here?"

"Waiting," she said, shifting her weight from one sneaker-clad foot to the other as though she were nervous or about to run away.

I closed the elevator cage behind me, unable to tear my eyes from the sight of her, my heart in my throat beating double time. God, it was so good to see her. She looked— "Amazing."

"No, waiting. I'm waiting. For you." She hurried forward, grabbing my duffel bag and carrying it to the door. "Did you have a nice flight? You look good. And tired. Good and tired."

"I am tired," I mumbled, picking up the rest of my stuff and following her down the hall, my eyes on her legs and backside as she strolled away and then bent to drop my duffel. If I'd been less exhausted, I would've had the presence of mind to avert my eyes. But she was wearing running shorts and her smooth, tan legs hijacked my attention. Abruptly, I was out of breath.

"Is it okay that I'm here?"

"What?" I croaked, blinking several more times as I forced my eyes to hers.

She looked worried. "I'm sorry, I know you're tired. Is this a problem?"

"What? No." I shook my head. "But why aren't you waiting *inside* my apartment?"

"I slipped the key under the door." She twisted her fingers in front of her, the smile she wore appeared agitated.

My attention flicked to the door, then back to her. "What's wrong? Why would you do that?"

She chewed on her bottom lip, and I almost groaned. *What I wouldn't give to—*

No.

No, no, no. I couldn't—wouldn't—think about that. I only allowed myself to indulge in these thoughts when I was alone, never with her. *Never with her.*

Her obvious and adorable consternation helped me refocus my attention. "I slipped it under your door because I didn't want to go back inside until you were home."

I breathed a short laugh. "What? Why?"

"I . . . think I . . . I don't want to say." She snapped her mouth shut as soon as the words were out.

I nodded and spoke around a yawn, "Fine. You don't want to say. When did you do this?" Alice often did things that made no sense to me, like hacking into my social media accounts and deleting messages she'd sent or storing life-size cutouts of Lord Byron and Ada Lovelace in my guest bedroom closet, and I'd learned to just roll with it. Life with Alice was never boring. "When did you slip the key under the door?"

"Yesterday."

"Oh. Okay. Well, come on in." I took a step closer, pulling my keys from my pants pocket, and Alice moved in front of me, her back pressed against the door, her arms slightly out from her sides as though barring the way.

"Don't you want me to unlock the door?" she asked, eyes wide. "You've been traveling for days. You're probably tired."

I took two steps back, my brain sluggish. I had been traveling all day, I hadn't showered since Nepal, and I probably stank, which meant I wasn't moving any closer to her. "I'm not too tired to unlock my door."

"But if I unlock it, then I can grab the key I left. I don't want you to—to accidentally slip on the key, since you're so tired."

"Fine." I shrugged, too tired to argue or question her motives. "If you want to unlock the door, go for it." I held up my keys.

She snatched them, and in the very next second, she'd turned to unlock the dead bolt, then the door, and then pushed inside. She also shut the door before I had a chance to follow.

What the—?

I waited for a minute, staring at the barricaded entrance, completely confused. I waited, figuring she'd open it once she realized she still had my keys and I couldn't get in. But after several moments, just when I'd lifted my hand to knock, she yanked the door open, a big smile on her face.

"There you are!" she said, like we'd been playing hide-and-seek.

I narrowed my eyes. Even for Alice, this was odd behavior.

"Why are you standing out there? Come in." She reached for my camera case and pulled the strap over my head. "Come in and relax." She set the case down just inside the apartment.

Expecting her to back up and allow me to pass, I was surprised when she instead shoved my keys at my chest, stepped into the hall and walked around me, heading for the stairwell.

"Wait—wait, Alice. Where are you going?" I turned, frowning at her retreat. "Aren't you staying?"

She also turned and faced me but continued to increase the distance between us, walking backward. "Oh, no. You're tired. I should go. I have things."

"Things?"

"Laundry. Mostly. A lot of laundry." She tilted her head back and forth. "Today is underwear day, so I can't miss that."

"No. Don't want to miss that." I pressed my lips together to keep from laughing. I was exhausted, but Alice could always make me laugh. I loved how honest she was, and I loved how it just spilled out of her. She'd *always* been this way. "What time tomorrow?"

"Oh, gosh." She glanced at her wrist, and I lifted an eyebrow because she had no watch on. She used to wear a watch but hadn't in years. "I think I have to work late tomorrow to make up for today, but I'm sure once you're settled, we will— well, I'll call."

"Okay." I nodded, bewildered. Maybe this whole interaction would make more sense after I slept.

"Okay! Bye!" With that, she turned and pushed through the stairwell door, disappearing.

I stared after her for a while hoping she'd come back. Maybe seconds, maybe minutes? I had no idea. When I caught myself, I zombie-walked into my apartment and shut the door. Shoving my luggage to one side, I set my keys on top of the hall table and shuffled to the kitchen, wanting some water. After that, a shower and nap.

On my way to the fridge, a new plant caught my attention, sitting on the kitchen table all by itself. The side of my mouth tugged upward at the sight of it in a little red ceramic pot. The leaves looked like big hearts and were green toward the bottom but pink and red near the top.

I sighed, making a mental note to look up how to take care of it. This one I wouldn't let die. I'd treat it right even if I had to take gardening lessons.

I was terrible at taking care of plants. I killed them, frequently, overwatering or underwatering or putting them in the wrong spot with too much or too little sun. But Alice had a green thumb. And keeping plants at my place gave me an excuse to give her a key, to ask her to check on the apartment and water the plants, to have her over after I returned.

I didn't care if that was sneaky and dishonest. Hey, whatever it took. I *needed* her in my life, and not to take care of houseplants.

Leaving the new heart plant where she'd left it, I scanned the potted greenery by the balcony door, the ones in the living room, and the orchid—another gift from Alice—on the entryway table. As always, everything looked great. Even more alive than when I'd left.

But then I spotted something on the floor by the front door. Crossing to it, I bent and picked it up.

It was a key.

The one I'd given to Alice.

PART THREE

MILO

Two days after I'd returned, she still hadn't called me. I'd texted her as soon as I'd woken up from my nap. She didn't respond. I'd texted again that night. Nothing.

I didn't want to bother her, and I figured she'd see the texts eventually. Anxious to see her and spend time together, I had to force myself not to text anything for three days. Besides, we'd likely run into each other on campus. She was a creature of habit, and I knew all her habits.

But at the end of the three days, when I hadn't seen her and she hadn't texted me, I sent her another message.

Milo: Can we meet at Palmer Hall for breakfast?

Alice: I can't! I'm working from home today.

Milo: Come over tonight or tomorrow or this weekend. I'll make you dinner.

She'd responded immediately.

Alice: I can't this week or weekend. Grant deadlines and dinner dates. But how about breakfast one day next week?

And that's it. *One day next week.* One day.

No asking how the trip had been, no random tidbit of information about *this day in history.* Nothing.

My mouth suddenly dry, I read the message maybe ten times, looking for a hidden meaning, but then I rolled my eyes at myself. That wasn't Alice. Alice didn't do hidden meanings; she didn't play games because she didn't know any. Alice said exactly what she meant all the time. It was one of the reasons I loved her so much.

Yet something felt off. I rubbed my fingers against a tight, uncomfortable sensation in my chest, trying to ignore it, and I texted her back,

Milo: I have work to do as well. Maybe we could work together? I can come to your place. Or when do you think you'll be free? I'll take you out if you don't want to eat my cooking. I miss you. I haven't seen you in months.

My thumb hovered over the *send* button for longer than I'd like to admit before I pressed it, reminding myself that, with Alice, I never had to pretend to be anything other than myself.

Well, except when you pretend you're not in love with her.

Gritting my teeth, I shoved that thought away.

It's not like I wanted to be dishonest about how I felt, how I'd always felt, from almost the very first moment she'd introduced herself in the tutoring lab going on fifteen years ago. Yes, she'd been beautiful. But more than that, she'd been friendly, open, kind, and patient. Being with her had been like being back in Iowa, and for a midwestern Italian boy living in New York, I couldn't get enough of her genuineness, her gorgeousness, or her company.

And did I mention she was brilliant? So fucking brilliant. I was convinced she thought in code, in equations and if-then statements. Her thought process was its own kind of artistry.

But I knew she hadn't felt the same about me. Even if she hadn't been engaged to that asshole—and then married that asshole, a moment I'd never quite recovered from—Alice didn't see me as anything but a friend.

That was fine. I would be her friend. I would always be her friend. If that's all she wanted from me, fine. It didn't change how much I adored her. I wanted—I'd always wanted—just to be in her orbit.

Tired of staring at the screen of my phone, rereading her last text and waiting for her to return mine, I shoved my cell in my back pocket and left my office in search of something to drink, maybe coffee, maybe tea. I wanted the walk more than I wanted the drink, which was why I skipped the stall at the bottom of the physics building and left campus.

On special occasions, Alice and I would walk to Tea and Sympathy in Greenwich Village. The owner was a real character, and all the dishes were mismatched, but I liked that the space was small, necessitating that we squeeze together no matter where we sat.

Deciding on tea, I turned in the direction of the tea shop, unable to cease ruminating on her last message. *I can't this week or weekend. Grant deadlines and dinner dates. But how about breakfast one day next week?*

One day next week?

It was the *one* in the message that I kept stumbling over. When I returned from my trips, even when she was still married to Will, we had breakfast every morning. I'd bring it to her office, or she'd bring it to mine; I'd make her crostata or panettone, my mother's recipes; she'd bake scones, cinnamon rolls, or coffee cake.

Opening the door to Tea and Sympathy, I lamented the lack of cinnamon rolls since my return. Did I mention she could bake? She could and did, often. For my birthday every year, she'd—

What. The. Fuck.

I halted just inside the door, my brain tripping on the sight of Alice sitting at a table next to a man, his arm along the back of her chair, his body angled toward hers, his eyes moving over her face and neck with unveiled appreciation.

I also halted because the tables were so crammed together it was difficult to navigate the space, even when it was empty. But even if it had been empty of everything except Alice and this dude, I suspected I wouldn't have been able to move.

Blood rushing between my ears, drowning out the crowd of patrons and their conversations, I watched Alice with the man, merciless to the warnings of my heart.

Look away.

Leave. Leave. Leave.

I couldn't.

He nuzzled her neck, and she allowed it. She allowed it. She didn't flinch away. She didn't tell him to get his damn hands off her. She faced him and smiled, and if an employee hadn't stepped in my field of vision, giving me a moment to process what I'd just seen, I might've broken the arm along the back of her chair.

"Dr. Magi," the girl said. She'd never been able to pronounce my last name, so I'd told her to call me *Magi*. "Hey. Are you here to meet Dr. Hooper?"

Struggling to swallow, I nodded dumbly. But then I shook my head. "I'm here for, uh—"

The man's laugh, loud and irritating, interrupted, making it hard to think or speak. Gritting my teeth and acting on pure instinct, I lifted my glare to Alice and her companion. At just that moment, she looked up, her eyes coming to mine, recognition and welcome lighting behind them, and I flinched at the impact. My heart spasmed like someone had wrapped their hands around the organ and squeezed.

"Milo!" She stood, waving me over, a big, gorgeous grin on her face.

Automatically, my feet carried me to her even as my brain told me to flee. *Leave. Leave. Leave.*

"Hey! Come sit with us." She gestured to the vacant seat across from hers. "Milo, this is Pete. He's getting his PhD in Fine Arts—"

"We're dating. I'm her boyfriend, she just hasn't gotten used to it yet," Pete said, his tone teasing as he interjected. He didn't stand, but instead lifted his hand for me to shake from where he sat.

I wanted to cut it off.

Alice huffed a laugh and continued, "Pete, this is Milo. He . . ." her voice trailed off, like she didn't know what label to assign or how to describe me.

"Ah, Milo." He smiled, small and wholly insincere, his hand still outstretched. "Alice talks about you all the time. Nice to meet you."

With an equally insincere grin pasted on my features and bitterness on my tongue, I took his offered hand and gave it a quick shake, determined not to squeeze too hard. I did not succeed. His smile fell, and he winced just before I released his fingers. *Good.*

Alice, looking a little flustered, tucked her hair behind her ears as she reclaimed her seat slowly, frowning. In the many moments that followed, she sipped her tea, opening and closing her mouth at intervals, as though trying to think of an appropriate topic of conversation given the animosity of our handshake and the fact that I hadn't taken the offered chair.

The stretching silence was tense, which, I admit, was completely my fault because I glared at her, refusing to help make this easy, refusing to pretend I was anything but insanely jealous.

I'd been good at hiding jealousy over the course of her marriage to Will the Asshole. It helped that I'd dated a lot. Or I'd tried to. When my inability to move past Alice became clear, I'd stopped dating, opting for women who wanted no-strings-attached hookups instead. I'd put an end to all that when Alice and Will split, and I hadn't been with anyone since.

It never settled well to think of myself in these terms, but I'd been biding my time. Waiting. Checking in at intervals to see if she was ready to date. *When she is*, I'd told myself, *I'll been ready. I'll make her love me.*

How fucking pathetic was I?

And now? Now that she was divorced from her cheating husband and had asserted for the last three years that she wasn't ready to date anyone? Now that she'd been unavailable or avoiding me for days? Now that I happen to stumble across her laughing and sharing a scone at *our* tea shop with Pete from the Fine Arts Department?

Yeah. Fuck pretending.

"Uh, so . . . how'd you two meet?" Pete's lips curled in a smile that resembled a sneer, clearing his throat, and returned his arm to the back of Alice's chair. I glared at his hand on her shoulder, the one I'd just squeezed too hard.

And fuck this guy.

"We go way back." My voice gruff, I volunteered this info before Alice could assemble her thoughts. "She tutored me in C++ when I was a grad student."

"He's my best friend," she said softly, her eyes coming to me but not quite making it past my neck. She could tell I was angry; she always had trouble meeting my eyes when I was angry. Suddenly assaulted by a stab of guilt, I glanced away, working to rein in my anger.

She doesn't owe you one goddamn thing, Milo.

I didn't want to make her uncomfortable. I didn't want to make her upset. And I didn't want to feel like a piece of garbage. Unfortunately, in this moment, I'd failed at all three.

I needed to leave.

"Well"—I backed away, shoving my hands in my pockets—"I'll see you around."

Always a glutton for punishment, I looked at her just as her eyes flickered to mine and then away.

"Yes. I'll—I'll message you about getting together for breakfast next week," she said with forced cheerfulness, and I wondered if it was for my benefit or for Pete's.

Does it matter?

Fighting a bitter smile, I dropped my chin to my chest so she wouldn't see my face and nodded. "Sure. Whenever. No rush," I said, then I turned away.

Pushing out of the café on autopilot, I walked toward my office but decided halfway there that I would leave for the day. I would walk over to Central Park. Maybe I'd go to the Met, lose myself in the samurai rooms.

I thought back to her last message when three blocks became ten blocks, the one I'd read at least twenty times, looking for a hidden meaning. *I can't,* she'd said. *Grant deadlines and dinner dates.*

Dinner dates.

I laughed, a sound devoid of all humor. Dinner dates had been precisely what she meant. Dinner dates. Dinner dates with Pete. *How long have they been together? Are they—*

The thought choked me, and I removed myself from pedestrian traffic, leaning against the cool concrete of a skyscraper, and closed my eyes. It didn't really matter where I went. I was a fool. A complete and total idiot.

And there was no escaping that.

PART FOUR

ALICE

I wasn't sure what to do.

Milo wasn't returning my text messages, emails, or calls. I wasn't pressuring him, just messaging once a week, trying to check in. After the first month, I'd cut down to once every two weeks. After three months, I asked my sister Jackie what to do, showing her our last exchanges and explaining that he'd been in a foul mood in the tea shop the last time I'd seen him.

"And you were there with someone else? With that Pete guy?"

I nodded, frowning at my phone and scrolling through the messages again for approximately the one thousandth time. "I wasn't avoiding him when he got back from Nepal. I just—" I huffed, tossing my phone to her couch. "I needed a minute to recalibrate things, you know? And to make plans with Pete, see where that went."

"Ugh, that guy." Jackie flopped down next to my phone on the couch, scooping it back up and typing in my passcode. "Has he finally taken the hint?"

"Yes. Thankfully." I flopped down next to her, peering over my shoulder as she pulled up Milo's last message to me. My heart gave a sad little twist. "I just wish I knew what I did wrong."

"Hmm." She twisted her lips to the side. "I don't know. I mean, he said he missed you and then didn't call you back? You don't need those kinds of mind games."

Crossing my arms, I tore my eyes away from the screen. I wasn't convinced Milo was playing mind games. We'd known each other for so many years, *so many*, and he'd never done this before. "I'm worried about him."

"What can you do? He won't return any of your calls." She passed the phone back to me, depositing it on my lap.

"I could go to his office."

"Don't do that. Don't show up where he works. If you're determined to see him, go to his apartment. Less chance of causing a scene if something really is wrong. But I think it's mind games, and you should ignore it. Ignore him."

I considered this advice, biting my thumbnail. "I've decided relationships aren't for me."

Jackie twisted toward me, angling her body. "Oh, really? Because of Milo's mind games?"

"No." I shook my head. "Dates. Several dates. Actually, fifty dates in the last two months."

She reared back. "Wait, what?"

I slid my eyes to hers. "You helped me set up that dating profile, remember? I told you I was going on dates."

"Jeez, Alice! I knew you'd been going on a lot of dates, but has it been fifty?" Her mouth hung open.

"It has. This morning was my fiftieth. And I think I'm done."

"What? No. You just need to—"

"Nope. I'm done."

"Okay, I'll bite." She huffed, rolling her eyes. "Why are you done?"

"Because I feel worse about myself after each date. I feel ugly and insufficient; I feel more awkward and oblivious. These dates, every single one of them, has made me feel like I'm an inferior human, and I don't want to do it anymore. Nothing can be worth the torment of that." *And Milo never made me feel that way and I miss him and, dammit, everything sucks.*

"Oh, honey." She pried one of my arms away from where I'd wrapped it over my stomach and cradled my hand. "It's hard out there, I know. But you have to just—"

"No." Withdrawing my hand from hers, I grabbed my phone and stood. "I'm done with romantic relationships, and I'm tired of waiting for Milo to text me back. You're right."

"Wait, how am I right?"

"I should go over to his apartment. Now."

"What about movie night? I was going to order Ethiopian food." She trailed after me to the door.

"I'll pick up dinner and take it to his place, then he can't turn me away. You can't turn away someone if they've bought you dinner. At least that's what all my dates have said."

"Oh my God, Alice. No. Your dates were wrong. You can most definitely turn someone away if they've bought you dinner. You haven't been letting these guys treat you badly, have you?"

"No. I've been splitting the cost of dinner so I can turn them away. Do you think Milo would want Ethiopian? Or tacos?"

She caught my hand just as I pulled my purse strap to my shoulder. "Stop for a moment. This is a bad idea."

"No. It's a good idea." I peeled her hand away after giving it a squeeze. "I'm not going to profess my love or anything. No, that business is all behind me."

"But you're letting him manipulate you."

"What? No. I'm worried about a friend. My best friend. I'm checking on him because I love him, as a friend." Maybe if I said it enough I'd believe it.

"You're going to fall back into bad habits."

"Nope. None of our habits were bad. I'm reclaiming a friendship that made me feel valued and good about myself. I've accepted he and I will always be friends and just friends, and I am honestly okay with that because I'd rather have a friendship with Milo than a romantic shit show with anyone else. And that's all that's out there. Shit shows."

Jackie winced, like my words pained her. "Alice, I'm so sorry. I feel like I need to apologize. When I told you to see people, to put yourself out there, I didn't mean for you to get hurt."

"Nah. I'm not hurt." I gave my sister a reassuring smile as I opened the door to her apartment. "It was a good lesson to learn. I'm glad I did it. Truly."

So I'd never have to do it again.

I picked up tacos.

First, they were faster. Second, serendipity put a taco food truck in my path, just two blocks from Jackie's apartment. Clearly, it was a sign. A taco sign.

Carrying my paper bag, I speed-walked to Milo's place, praying he'd be there and making a plan for the likely scenario that he was gone on a trip. Or on a date. *Or has a woman over.*

Ugh. The thought hurt, but I would get over it. He'd never introduced me to anyone, and I'd never seen him with a woman, not even at my wedding. Which was why it was so easy for me to believe he never dated. But Jackie was right all those months ago. Milo must've dated over the last fifteen years, or at least had hookups. I would be naïve to think otherwise.

And, honestly, it was none of my business. His love life was not my concern. If he didn't want to share details with me, fine. Part of me was grateful he'd kept our friendship separate from his hookups, especially after the divorce as my feelings had grown and swelled and matured.

Marching up the stairs to his building, I smiled at the doorman—who I recognized—and lifted up the bag. "Taco night."

"Oh, lucky guy." Frank winked, opening the door. "Great timing, he just got back."

I stopped just before the doorway. "He just got back?"

"You know, from his run?" Frank's eyes widened.

"Oh! Yes. From his run." I grinned, nodding. "Right. Sorry. Thanks, Frank!" Continuing into the building, I made a beeline for the stairs and ended up taking them two at a time, working off a bit of my nervous energy.

By the time I made it to his door, I was out of breath, but I banged on it anyway. I'd been playing it safe with Milo. I'd been hiding my feelings, worried I would lose him. It had never occurred to me that I might lose him anyway. *Perhaps a little recklessness is in order.*

I heard the faint sound of approaching footsteps and then a pause. I knew he was looking through the peephole, so I lifted up the bag of tacos, giving his door a stern glare. "I know you're in there. I have tacos," I said, but didn't add, *And I'm not afraid to use them.*

I felt his hesitation. Seconds stretched. I swallowed, glaring at the door, tempted to knock again. But thankfully, I didn't have to.

Milo opened the door—not wide but not a crack either—and leveled me with a look that felt reluctant. "Alice."

"Is this a bad time?"

"Uh—"

"If this is a bad time, I can leave. I brought tacos, but I will leave them here if you want them. Basically, they're no-pressure tacos. They are yours regardless of whether you want me to stay."

He exhaled something that sounded a little like a laugh and blinked several times, taking a step back. Milo's green eyes moved between me and the bag of tacos and I could see I'd truly surprised him. He didn't seem to know what to say.

Rather than continue to stand silently outside his apartment waiting for him to gather his wits, I pressed on, "I'm serious. No pressure if you just want the tacos. It's just, I'm worried about you."

His gaze darted back to mine and narrowed. "Why are you worried about me?"

"Because you're ignoring me."

He grimaced, his attention dropping to the floor. "I'm not—I haven't been ignoring you."

That statement was patently false and sounded like code, so I said, "No, you have definitely been ignoring me. But it's okay. I can live with you ignoring me if I know you're okay. Are you okay?"

His mouth was flat as he brought his eyes back to mine and gave me a short, stiff nod. "I'm okay."

I stared at him, openly assessing. He stared at me, looking guarded. When this continued for many seconds, I nodded, my stomach sinking.

"Okay, okay. If you're okay, then I guess I'll be going. Do you want the tacos?"

Milo's stare grew less guarded and more . . . something else. Something I couldn't define. Distracted maybe? Frustrated? It was a look I didn't recognize, so I waited for his answer.

At length, he sighed loudly and stepped back from the door. "Come in, Alice. We'll have tacos."

I clutched the bag to my chest protectively. "Are you sure? I don't want to force my tacos on you. I did not come here to make you eat unwanted tacos."

The side of his mouth curved, just the slightest fraction of an inch, and his handsome green eyes twinkled at me, just the slightest fraction of twinkle. But the sight made my heart go flip-flop and my sinking stomach reverse course.

"I'm starving, and I want your tacos. I want your tacos real bad."

I grinned, resisting the urge to *squeee*. Instead I nodded and stepped into Milo's apartment. He took the bag, turning away and crossing to the kitchen table as I closed the door.

"Do you want something to drink?" He placed the bag on the table next to a big glass of water. "Tea? Water? *Wine?*"

The word *wine* came out weird—or at least it sounded weird to me—all sardonic and brittle, like wine was code for something else.

Maybe that's why I said, "Yeah. Sure. I'll take some wine."

Milo glanced at me over his shoulder, a single eyebrow raised. "Really?"

"Yes, really." I smiled in spite of his weirdness. It was such a relief to see Milo, spend time with him, be near him. If he wanted to be weird, I'd let him be weird.

"Okay." He said the word haltingly, his eyebrow lift persisting, and crossed to the sideboard where he had a tabletop wine rack.

Meanwhile, I watched him move. I watched his long fingers pull a bottle from the rack. I watched his strong hands hold it. I watched his dark curly hair fall over his forehead and his achingly handsome profile as he studied the label.

Who am I kidding? I'm not watching, I'm admiring. I might even be lusting.

And I couldn't stop. My eyes traveled over his broad shoulders, his bared bicep and arm, his tapered waist and hip and long, lean legs. Mouth suddenly dry, I wished I'd asked for water. But it was too late. Milo had already started opening the bottle, cutting away the foil at the top.

I tore my gaze away, telling myself I hadn't come here to ogle him, and forced my attention to survey the apartment. It was just the same, just the—

"Wait a minute." I frowned, my head turning toward the patio door, the entryway table, the corner of the living room. "Where are all your plants?"

Milo's back straightened and he rolled his shoulders, momentarily pausing his progress with the wine bottle, but he didn't look at me. "I—uh—I gave them away."

"You . . ." All the breath left my lungs, forced out. He'd knocked the wind out of me.

He snuck a quick look in my direction, the line of his mouth stern. "Yes. I gave them away. All of them."

"I see," I said weakly, my eyes dropping to the floor, my brain rioting. "I see."

But I didn't see.

I'd given him those plants. He'd said he loved them. He'd said he loved that they reminded him of me. He'd said he would always take care of them. And he'd given them away?

I couldn't think past this news, which was probably why I blurted, "Why would you do that?"

Milo chuckled, shaking his head. It was not a friendly sound, and it confused me. "Come on, Alice. We both know it was never going to happen."

This sounded like more code. "What wasn't going to happen?"

"I was never—am never—" He waved a hand in the air, as though looking for the right words. "I'm never going to be good at taking care of houseplants. It was time to, you know, face reality."

More and more and more code. But unlike computer code, this was a cipher I couldn't solve. "So you gave them away? To whom?"

"Carly."

"Carly?" I blinked rapidly. "Do I know her?"

"You don't know all my friends." He shrugged, the words dismissive.

I continued staring at him, watching him. This time not with admiration but with worry. An odd, unpleasant sensation took up residence in my stomach. Something was wrong.

"Are you sure you're okay?"

"I'm fine. You want to unpack the food?" His voice flat, he finished uncorking the bottle and reached for two glasses, setting them on the sideboard. They were huge, and he filled them almost to the top.

"Oh no." I stepped forward, walking to the table. "Milo, that's too much for me. If I drink all that, I'll have to stay the night."

"You know you can stay any time you want." He walked around the table to the kitchen, throwing away the cork and foil while saying something under his breath I didn't catch.

"What was that?" I opened the bag of tacos. Oddly, I was no longer hungry.

"Unless your boyfriend minds," he said much louder and firmer, nearly a shout.

"My boyfriend?" I didn't have a boyfriend. *Why would he think I have a boyfriend?*

Not looking at me, he returned to the sideboard and picked up the wineglasses, placing them on the table. "Yes. You know, your date."

My date . . . ? I didn't have a date tonight. I'd decided to stop all that nonsense, but Milo knew nothing about that since we hadn't talked in months. "I don't have a date."

He claimed his seat at the head of the table, accepting the wrapped taco I held without meeting my eyes. "I'm talking about the guy you were dating after I got back from Nepal."

"Oh! Peter?" I grimaced. That was so long ago. "Blah. No. He's not my boyfriend."

"Oh?" He peered at me while unwrapping his dinner.

"No. No, we just went on the one date and then he wouldn't leave me alone." Going through the motions, I took the chair next to his and unwrapped my taco, even though I had no plans to eat it. "I actually had to get campus police involved. It was an unpleasant experience."

Milo grew very still, and his stillness had me glancing at him.

"Just the one date?"

"Yes."

His eyes moved over me, his eyebrows pulling together. "And then he stalked you?"

"No. Not stalk. Not really." I leaned back in my seat and crossed my arms, thinking back over my last few months. "More like, he kept coming to my office even after I told him I was no longer interested, wanting to chat and saying we should be friends. When I made it clear I didn't want to be friends, he kept doing it anyway. And then it got awkward when he followed me as I met a different date and then watched me the whole night from his table across the restaurant."

"Wait. Wait a minute." Milo held up a hand and scrunched his face, making me think I'd confused him. "He stalked you?"

I grimaced. "No. More like hovered, unwelcome, in a creepy fashion."

"Stalked."

Waving away the word, I sighed. "Whatever. Anyway, that's done. He's stopped and all other dating is at an end."

"Other dating?"

"Yes." I chuckled. "It's been an interesting few months, and there have been a lot of dates, all bad. Some horrifying."

"What do you mean *a lot of dates*?"

"Jackie helped me set up an online dating profile and I went on a lot of dates." I picked up my wineglass and watched him stare at me over the rim as I took a sip. That odd, unpleasant feeling in my stomach unfurled and then swirled, making the wine taste sour. "I don't really want to talk about it, and it's irrelevant now anyway."

"What do you mean irrelevant? Why is it irrelevant?" Milo moved to the edge of his seat, having no problem making eye contact now. In fact, he seemed engrossed. "Did you . . . find someone?"

"No. Not at all. And that's why it's irrelevant." I set the wineglass on the table. "I've decided you have the right philosophy on these matters."

He squinted, his eyes moving back and forth like he was rummaging through his brain, searching for his philosophy.

"I no longer believe in relationships," I filled in, giving my shoulders a little shrug.

Everything about him went still again, eerily still, and he looked at me. He just simply *looked.*

I glanced at him, then away, then at him again. I reached for and took another sip of my wine. I set the glass on the table, nudging it farther away from me with my fingers. His look turned into another stare as he sat on the edge of his seat, his eyes narrowed, his lips parted as though words were gathering on the tip of his tongue.

He held so still and stared at me for so long, I felt prompted to ask again, "Are you sure you're okay?"

He sighed, closing his eyes as though exhausted, and his breathing seemed to grow labored. "Actually, no. I'm not okay. I'm not okay." He leaned back in the chair and covered his face with both hands. It took me a minute to realize that his shoulders were shaking, and another few seconds to determine if he was laughing or crying.

"Are . . . are you laughing?"

"Oh yes." He nodded, his hands still covering his face. "I am laughing."

I felt my eyebrows pull together. "Did I do something funny?"

His hands slid away, he gathered a slow, deep breath, lifted his eyes to mine, and glared. I flinched. He looked mad. Really mad. His jaw ticked and his usually smiling lips were curved in an unhappy frown.

"Alice," he said.

Now I held very still. "Milo."

"I love you."

I studied him, pressing my lips together as I considered what he might mean by this statement. "You love me," I repeated, turning the words over and over, another coded message.

Usually, in ye times of old, I wouldn't have done this with Milo. He was the one person I'd never had to do this with. But tonight he was acting strange, and he wasn't okay but kept insisting he was, and I felt like secret messages were everywhere.

He nodded, still looking positively irate.

"I . . . love you . . . too," I said. We'd never said this to each other before. Some friends did, but it was a first for us. And it wasn't a lie to say I loved him. I did.

My response only seemed to infuriate him further, and he grit his teeth. "No, Alice."

"Yes, Milo." Abruptly, I became aware that I was nodding and likely had been for a while. So I put a stop to that.

Milo continued to glare, blinking rapidly, as if I'd blown dust in his eyes or he was absorbing some bad news. At least that's what I thought the look on his face meant.

"As a friend?" he ground out, making the word *friend* sound like it really meant *toxic waste* which only served to further baffle me.

"What's wrong with being friends?" I felt my head begin to move in a nod and quickly put a stop to it.

He flinched, seemed to struggle around a swallow for a moment, and leaned forward again, placing his forearm and hand on the table, his fingers just two inches from my wineglass, which he stared at, and said, "What if I told you that's not what I want?"

He doesn't want to be my friend? Was that what this was all about? Was that why he'd ghosted me? I was going to cry. I could feel it.

Don't cry.

Before I could sort myself out, he asked, "What if I told you I'm in love with you?"

I recoiled at the blunt force of his hypothetical question, and my frown was immediate. Something in the vicinity of my chest ached—my heart—and my ears rang. We regarded each other, and the ache in my heart became a hurt, a wound. Now I was the one breathing hard.

"What the hell is going on?" I demanded.

"Alice—"

"Are you making fun of me?"

He shook his head, some of the anger dissolving, leaving his features pained. "I'm in love with you, Alice."

I recoiled again, closing my eyes because I couldn't look at him right now *and* make my body move. "Very funny, Milo," I mumbled, standing and blindly walking to the vicinity of the door. "Forget it. Forget I came over. You can keep the tacos."

I heard his chair scrape against the floor and his footsteps follow before I heard his raised voice close behind. "Why would you doubt it? How could I be any more obvious?"

"Oh, I don't know. You could always ask me on a date." I tried to keep my voice light, but I could feel tears gathering behind my eyes. "But that's right. You don't do relationships."

Had he found out? Did I leave a page of my letter behind? Why would he do this to me?

His hand caught mine, stopping me, and I tore it out of his grip, spinning to face him as an uncomfortable rush of heat pulsed through my body. "Don't touch me."

He held his hands up, taking just a half step back. He was no longer glaring, yet the intensity of his stare hadn't lessened. "Maybe this isn't something you want to hear, and maybe I'm ruining our friendship, and I don't want to do that. But I can't do *this* anymore."

"Do what?"

"Pretend I don't want more—" His eyes dropped to my lips, lowered to my neck, chest, stomach before he slammed them shut. "So much more with you." His eyes opened and hooked into mine. "I'm—I have been—in love with you for years. Before you and Will divorced. Hell, before you got married. And I thought —I hoped—" He stopped himself, swallowing thickly, his breath fast and shallow, his eyes darting between mine.

A crack of doubt opened up inside me, that maybe he was telling the truth?

Milo took another step back. "After you and Will split, you needed time, to heal and figure things out. And so I waited. I waited for you to be ready to date. And I waited for you. But—I know that's not fair, to put that on you. And—fuck, I'm messing this up."

He speared his hair with his fingers, his face contorting. And that crack of doubt widened into possibility.

"What are you saying to me?" I gained the step he'd retreated.

"I adore you. I think about you all the time. Being with no one, it hasn't been a hardship because I'd rather have a part of you then a whole of someone else. I'm in love with you and I want us to be together. I want you to give me a chance."

A shaking breath burst out of me and I covered my mouth, closing my eyes, afraid to look at him or speak or move because how could this possibly be happening? How could this be real?

"I'm sorry I was a dick tonight," he went on. "I was a giant, colossal, monster dick. I'm sorry. Please, please forgive me. No matter what you decide, if things can go back to the way they were and you can forget about this, if we can pretend it never happened, I would be fine with that. I would. I just want to—I want to know you, whatever that means for you."

How many times? How many times had I thought about this moment? Except I'd been the one spilling my guts. "I can't believe this is really happening."

"Are you . . . Have I ruined everything?"

"No!" I laughed even though my eyes were leaking, the emotions of the moment overwhelming, which made my voice unsteady. "No. Not at all. You're perfect."

I heard his breath hitch. I felt him move closer, his hands grabbing mine and pulling them away from my face.

"Alice." My name was a rough whisper, like it was torn from him, and in the next moment I stiffened because his lips brushed against mine. "God. Alice. Kiss me."

A burst of heat, a shock, pushed outward against my skin and I held my breath, my chin lifting an inch, searching, seeking. But an inch was all that was necessary for our mouths to meet, and a tremor went through me at the contact. He groaned, like the feel of my lips hurt, like it was torture. His arms surrounded me, holding me tight; his hands grabbed fistfuls of my shirt; and his tongue swept out to test the seam of my lips.

Immediately, I opened to him, for him. Not content with fabric, I filled my hands with him, his body. I touched what I'd so desperately admired earlier, mindlessly sliding my fingers under his exercise shirt to caress the shape and texture of his skin while he devoured me with teeth and tongue, hot and searching, savoring yet frantic, like he expected me to pull away, like he expected this to end.

I didn't become aware that we were walking until my back hit a wall and he rocked his hips against mine, a rhythmic movement that made me gasp, the hard length of him not quite where I needed.

"Milo!"

"I need you." His mouth trailed down my neck, kissing, nipping, sucking, tasting. His arms loosened as his hands mimicked mine, delving under my shirt to slide across my bare skin, lifting my shirt. "God, Alice. I need you so much."

Finally, *finally*, nothing about his words sounded like a puzzle or a code for me to break. They may have been spoken unintentionally, mindlessly, but they were real, raw, honest, and they stole my breath.

"Touch me," he demanded on a growl, capturing my hand and bringing it to the front of his shorts.

I did. I touched him. I stroked him through the thin layers of fabric, and he shuddered. He sucked in a shaky breath, pressing himself into my hand, lifting his chin to gaze into my eyes. Milo's typically jade green eyes were now emerald flames, and the exposed desire felt almost violent, a torrent of suppressed yearning that strangled me.

How had I not seen it before now? How had he hidden himself from me so completely? And why had he never told me?

I wanted to ask the questions circling around my head, but Milo had captured my mouth again, his kiss harder this time, hungry, and we were moving again. Pulling me from the wall, his hands at my thighs, hitching the hem of my skirt, his fingers hooked into my underwear. He steered us into his bedroom, kissing me, his tongue in my mouth an expert invasion, making me wild. I was surprised when the back of my knees hit the bed, and as we separated, as I fell backward, he pulled off my shirt in one fluid movement. His soon followed, then his shorts, and I lifted onto my elbows to watch him, to see him.

My mouth flooded with saliva, my eyes trailing over his gorgeous body. So beautiful. He was—everywhere—beauty. A single lamp on the nightstand cast his strong, lean, muscular body in shadowy, sharp relief as he reached for and rolled on a condom. I swallowed, my heart racing, but I wasn't given long to admire him before he moved above me, his eyes on mine, no longer merely hungry but ravenous.

He lifted my skirt, his fingers once more hooking into the waistband of my underwear before he tugged it down. I reached for him, wanting to touch him, feel his weight above me, but Milo retreated, watching the fabric slide along my legs, his expression dazed.

"I can't believe this is happening," he whispered, giving me the impression that he'd meant to think the words, not say them out loud. His eyes darted to mine, searching, the first flicker of uncertainty cutting through the haze of passion. "What are you thinking?"

My tongue flicked out to lick my lips, nerves and anticipation twisting together. I told myself not to let my gaze stray to his body. I told myself not to be distracted by the dazzling display of manly perfection that was Milo Manganiello. He was . . . God. Damn. He was so *hot*. And faced with the reality of him, who he was, I could see now that I'd been ignoring his beauty for years in favor of his mind and his heart.

I'd had his mind and his heart. He'd just confessed they'd been mine all along. I knew that now.

But his body . . .

"Alice," he whispered on a hitching breath, climbing over me slowly, the full weight and intensity of his gaze on my face, searching. "What are you thinking?"

My thoughts? I couldn't give voice to them. They felt too sharp, too clumsy.

I love you.

I'm in love with you.

I can't believe this is happening either.

Please, never leave me. Never hurt me.

No, I couldn't say any of that. Not yet.

But I did ask, "Why?" choking on the word and my emotions. "Why didn't you tell me?"

Milo's chest rose and fell with shallow breaths, the emerald of his gaze growing darker. "You weren't mine and I didn't want to lose you," he said, his eyes closing as his forehead fell to the mattress. "Fuck, Alice. I can't lose you."

"You have me," I said, turning my head to kiss his neck, draw his earlobe into my mouth, my hands shaking as they touched his sides, his back, then smoothed down to his bare hips.

"Do I?" The question sounded strangled, and he lifted his head again. He supported his weight on one arm and his other hand moved between my legs. As soon as he touched me, as soon as his finger sought and found my center, we both sucked in a breath, the crown of my head pressing against the mattress. "Do I have you?"

I nodded. "Yes. Always." The words were more than a breath but less than a whisper. I couldn't think because he was stroking me, his hot, heavy erection pressing against the inside of my thigh.

Holding my stare, his lit with renewed hunger but also desperation. "Promise me."

"I promise," I managed, my hands kneading his body, grabbing as my hips rolled, seeking more of his touch. "Milo," I whimpered, lifting my chin to take his mouth.

He withheld it even as his stomach muscles flexed in a lithe movement, making me wild, removing his hand and positioning himself at my entrance. "Do you need me like I need you?"

I tried to swallow but I couldn't, my throat didn't work, and I barely managed to croak out, "You know I do. I'm—I'm so in love with you."

Milo's eyes widened, his lips parting in what looked like surprise, and then his mouth fastened to mine. He filled me with a forceful stroke. He groaned. I gasped, exposing my throat, my body arching, straining to meet his.

God. It felt so good. He felt so good. So good. He felt like heaven. His body heavy, hot, strong, demanding. His eyes cherishing and greedy. Lifting himself, he tugged down the strap of my bra and my fumbling fingers helped, unhooking the clasp at the front. He cursed, looking almost angry as his eyes blazed over my lips, chin, neck, and breasts.

"You are so fucking beautiful," he said, sounding breathless.

"So are you." I tilted my hips, feeling as though I might go mad with the slow, measured friction.

Something inside him seemed to settle at the mindless nature of my words and he lowered himself again, capturing my lips once more, the slide of his tongue an echo of his invasion. This time I shuddered as he plunged deeper, harder, his mouth voracious and skilled.

I was so close, racing toward my crisis. My blood pumping hot and thick, heat pooling low in my abdomen, a heavy knot, my mind barely keeping up with the reality of what we were doing, what was happening.

"I love you," I whispered between his greedy kisses, the words cracking, arriving broken. So much feeling, so many hopes and wishes I'd been too afraid to share. I closed my eyes, again overwhelmed, and fighting tears I couldn't name.

"Oh God, Alice. I'm—" He spoke through gritted teeth, his hand moving from my hip to the front of my body, his thumb stroking in time with his thrusts, and I lost all ability to think or breathe. My body took over, my hips pivoting grace-lessly as stars burst behind my eyes, a cry rang from my throat, and the pooling, twisting heat in my abdomen swelled and surged, a torrent of pleasure and pain and heaven and bliss.

I knew he was also coming, his hands grasping, his mouth swallowing my cries as a feral-sounding groan tore out of him. I felt the riotous thrum and thump of Milo's heart against my breast as he moved, his strokes rough and covetous, his thighs flexing as he pushed me up the bed until he slowed and stilled.

Kissing me, he rolled to his side, bringing me with him, wrapping me in his strong arms and holding me as though I might escape or disappear. In truth, I felt so fucking awesome, happy and satisfied and used and replete, I might've been in danger of floating away had he not anchored my body to his.

Separating our lips, he settled my cheek against his chest, and we took a moment to catch our breath. All at once I became aware his fingers were in my hair at my temple, sifting through it softly, reverently. His other hand stroked up and down my body in a languid movement, as though petting me, and it felt so good, so necessary. I stretched like a cat and sighed happily.

But he was silent. And I couldn't discern if he was content or troubled, and the not knowing plagued me.

He said he loves you, he's in love with you. Relax. I felt myself tense.

You know him. He's your best friend. Calm down. My mind was in chaos.

Abruptly, I wondered if he regretted it, and I hated the thought. But it wouldn't go away. He'd left me, ignored me, gave away all his plants—all our plants—and what if—

"Alice. What are you thinking?" Milo's voice sounded gravelly, rough, maybe a little stern.

I squeezed my eyes shut.

Slowly, I felt him draw back, push me away just a little. "Look at me."

By force of will alone, I opened my eyes, but I couldn't lift them higher than the perfection of his tanned neck. "I want—" I started, stopped, sucked in a breath for courage around my heart lodged in my throat, and tried again. "I want you to get those plants back."

Milo held perfectly still, and I felt the weight of his stare. Inhaling another deep breath, I lifted my eyes to his, bracing myself. But when our gazes met, his was so warm, so loving.

The side of his mouth hitched, and he nodded, threading his fingers through mine and bringing them to his lips. "I will buy you a whole greenhouse of houseplants. I will buy you a whole damn farm if you want. If you agree to marry me."

Tears stung my eyes, my heart swelling in my chest, and I returned his slow spreading smile, nodding before I was fully aware what I was doing. "A whole damn farm?" I asked, laughing a little.

"That's right. A whole damn farm," he confirmed, his eyes liquid with emotion, open and earnest. "In exchange for promising me forever and never letting me go."

Instead of answering with words, and because now he was mine—mind, heart, and body—I kissed him. And I never let him go.

THE END

ABOUT THE AUTHOR

Penny Reid is the *New York Times, Wall Street Journal,* and *USA Today* Best-selling Author of the Winston Brothers, Knitting in the City, Rugby, Dear Professor, and Hypothesis series. She used to spend her days writing federal grant proposals as a biomedical researcher, but now she just writes books. She's also a full time mom to three diminutive adults, wife, daughter, knitter, crocheter, sewer, general crafter, and thought ninja.

Come find me -
Mailing List: http://pennyreid.ninja/newsletter/
Goodreads: http://www.goodreads.com/ReidRomance
Facebook: www.facebook.com/pennyreidwriter
Instagram: www.instagram.com/reidromance
Twitter: www.twitter.com/reidromance
Patreon: https://www.patreon.com/smartypantsromance
Email: pennreid@gmail.com ...hey, you! Email me ;-)

OTHER BOOKS BY PENNY REID

Knitting in the City Series

(Interconnected Standalones, Adult Contemporary Romantic Comedy)

Neanderthal Seeks Human: A Smart Romance (#1)

Neanderthal Marries Human: A Smarter Romance (#1.5)

Friends without Benefits: An Unrequited Romance (#2)

Love Hacked: A Reluctant Romance (#3)

Beauty and the Mustache: A Philosophical Romance (#4)

Ninja at First Sight (#4.75)

Happily Ever Ninja: A Married Romance (#5)

Dating-ish: A Humanoid Romance (#6)

Marriage of Inconvenience: (#7)

Neanderthal Seeks Extra Yarns (#8)

Knitting in the City Coloring Book (#9)

Winston Brothers Series

(Interconnected Standalones, Adult Contemporary Romantic Comedy, spinoff of Beauty and the Mustache)

Beauty and the Mustache (#0.5)

Truth or Beard (#1)

Grin and Beard It (#2)

Beard Science (#3)

Beard in Mind (#4)

Dr. Strange Beard (#5)

Beard with Me (#6)

Beard Necessities (#7)

Winston Brothers Paper Doll Book (#8)

Hypothesis Series

(New Adult Romantic Comedy Trilogies)

Elements of Chemistry: ATTRACTION, HEAT, and CAPTURE (#1)

Laws of Physics: MOTION, SPACE, and TIME (#2)

Irish Players (Rugby) Series – by L.H. Cosway and Penny Reid

(Interconnected Standalones, Adult Contemporary Sports Romance)

The Hooker and the Hermit (#1)

The Pixie and the Player (#2)

The Cad and the Co-ed (#3)

The Varlet and the Voyeur (#4)

Dear Professor Series

(New Adult Romantic Comedy)

Kissing Tolstoy (#1)

Kissing Galileo (#2)

Ideal Man Series

(Interconnected Standalones, Adult Contemporary Romance Series of Jane Austen Reimaginings)

Pride and Dad Jokes (#1, coming 2022)

Man Buns and Sensibility (#2, TBD)

Sense and Manscaping (#3, TBD)

Persuasion and Man Hands (#4, TBD)

Mantuary Abbey (#5, TBD)

Mancave Park (#6, TBD)

Emmanuel (#7, TBD)

Handcrafted Mysteries Series

(A Romantic Cozy Mystery Series, spinoff of *The Winston Brothers Series*)

Engagement and Espionage (#1)

Marriage and Murder (#2)

Home and Heist (#3, coming 2022)

Baby and Ballistics (#4, coming 2023)

Pie Crimes and Misdemeanors (TBD)

Good Folks Series

((Interconnected Standalones, Adult Contemporary Romantic Comedy, spinoff of *The Winston Brothers Series*)

Totally Folked (#1, coming 2021)

Give a Folk (#2, coming 2022)

Three Kings Series

(Interconnected Standalones, Holiday-themed Adult Contemporary Romantic Comedies)

Homecoming King (#1, coming Christmas 2021)

Drama King (#2, coming Christmas 2022)

Prom King (#3, coming Christmas 2023)

CPSIA information can be obtained
at www.ICGtesting.com
Printed in the USA
BVHW082210250721
612853BV00006B/65